A Sound to Remember

PICTURES BY GABRIEL LISOWSKI

A Sound to Remember

BY SONIA LEVITIN

HARCOURT BRACE JOVANOVICH   NEW YORK AND LONDON

LIBRARY OF CONGRESS CATALOGING IN PUBLICATION DATA
Levitin, Sonia, 1934-
   A sound to remember.
SUMMARY: Jacov, a slow boy, is given the special
honor of "blowing the shofar (ram's horn)" on the
Jewish high holy days.
[1. Jews—Rites and ceremonies—Fiction]
I. Lisowski, Gabriel.   II. Title.
PZ7.L58So   [E]   79-87522
ISBN 0-15-277248-0

First edition
B C D E

FOR RABBI LEON M. KAHANE, WHO MADE IT HAPPEN

Long ago, in the distant land of our fathers, lived a boy named Jacov. He was a fine boy, but slow of speech and a bit clumsy, so that some of the villagers made him an object of scorn.

The other boys sometimes teased him and
whispered about him behind their hands. Some
men of the village tapped their heads when Jacov
went by. Even a few of the good wives were known

to cluck-cluck about Jacov should he chance
to stumble in their path or stutter a greeting.

Now, the village rabbi was a
teacher to all who studied and
a friend to all who sought
goodness. To Jacov he was both
teacher and friend. In the
village it was thought that
the rabbi could do no
wrong. He was blessed
for his kindness and
praised for his wisdom.

The week before Rosh
Hashanah, the Jewish
New Year, the rabbi
announced the name of
the one who would hold
the singular honor of
blowing the shofar, the
ram's horn. When the
people heard the name,
they were astounded.
Who should blow the
shofar on the day of Rosh
Hashanah? None else,
declared the rabbi,
but Jacov.

The elders of the congregation approached the rabbi, heads respectfully bowed. They asked the rabbi, could he have made a mistake? Did the rabbi really intend to entrust this holy task to Jacov?

Yes. Jacov was indeed to blow the shofar.

Then the women of the congregation approached the rabbi, murmuring softly, eyes modestly downcast. Wouldn't the rabbi reconsider and choose one of the elders instead?

No, thank you. Jacov was going to blow the shofar.

Other boys of the congregation approached
the rabbi, each submitting his own name. Each
recited his virtues and his good deeds,
begging to be chosen.

But the rabbi was resolute. The shofar would be
sounded by Jacov.

On the eve of Rosh Hashanah, before the sun
had set, Jacov himself stood before the rabbi. His
face was aglow with joy, but his hands trembled
and his speech faltered.

"D-d-do you really think I—I am the right one
to b-b-blow the shofar?"

The rabbi placed his hand on Jacov's head.
"You shall blow the shofar, Jacov. I wish it, and
so too, I believe, it will be pleasing to God."

"B-but what if I make a mistake?"

The rabbi said softly, "In such matters, Jacov,
there can be no mistake. Allow God to guide
you. All will be well."

Now the rabbi reminded Jacov that this year the
first day of Rosh Hashanah happened to fall on the
Sabbath. "We may not blow the shofar on the
Sabbath," he said, "so you will only blow it on the
second day of Rosh Hashanah."

He smiled. "Our eagerness to hear it will be
even greater."

Thus the first day of Rosh Hashanah came and went.

On the second day Jacov again put on his Bar Mitzvah suit and his dark shoes, which were polished to a high gloss. His mother and father, dressed in their holiday best, their faces shining with pride, could not seem to take their eyes off Jacov.

Their son! Their son had been chosen to blow the shofar on Rosh Hashanah. It was an honor to remember one's whole life long.

In the synagogue everything was in readiness. The congregation was seated. A hush of expectancy seemed to hang in the air. This was the birthday, according to Scripture, the birthday of the world. This day was the solemn beginning of the ten days of awe, wherein God's children remember their holy purpose to do right, to love Him, and to renew their faith.

All through the service there lay the undercurrent of anticipation. Soon would come the high point—

the clear, strong call of the ram's horn, sounding like no other instrument on earth, calling out, "Hark! Listen! It is time to repent, time to renew, time to become at one with your God!"

Jacov, sitting near the rabbi on the bemah, felt his throat tighten. Each year of his life he had sat down among the congregation, waiting for another to blow the horn. Now, incredibly, Jacov was the figure upon whom all eyes were turned as he walked toward the pulpit, shofar in his hand.

He had practiced, of course, for many hours. He had learned how to control his breathing, how to bring the sound out from the horn to spread far, far and long. He had learned how to press his lips firmly but also gently around the mouthpiece, how to guide the notes from low to high until there came that stirring sound, causing hearts to beat faster as the notes pierced the air, calling, commanding, consoling all the people, proclaiming, "All's well! We are gathered, we of Israel, and God is here!"

Now Jacov lifted the horn. He had not known that his hands would tremble so! He had not known that his throat would tighten, his chest feel hollow, his mouth dry as sand.

The rabbi called out the first tones. *"Tekiah!"*

With an effort, Jacov brought the shofar to his lips. In his mind he imagined the notes almost like living things, with bodies and spirits of their own. Yes, the notes would dance and fill the synagogue like ringing bells.

But as Jacov blew, the only sound that came was a faint, dry crackling tone.

"Shvarim!" rang out the rabbi's cry.

Jacov blew the shofar in response, wishing it would be the beautiful and inspiring call he so desired to give to his parents, to the congregation, and most of all to his friend the rabbi.

Out came the notes, weak and trembling.
Better than the first attempt, at least these notes
were adequate. Jacov felt his palms sweating.

He had one more chance to make the shofar sing on this Rosh Hashanah day.

Now came the rabbi's chant, *"Teruah!"*

Jacov blew. From the shofar came not a sound. He felt the rabbi's eyes upon him, waiting. The eyes of the congregation, too, seemed to pierce through him. Again Jacov blew. Still the shofar remained silent.

Jacov stole a glance at the rabbi. Gently the rabbi nodded, urging Jacov to try again.

With all his might Jacov struggled, but he
could not fight the panic he felt. He closed his
eyes, hard. Desperately he blew once more,
wishing with all his heart to make the shofar ring.

From the shofar came nothing. Not a sound.

A sigh swept over the congregation, followed by
a low rumble and angry frowns. They had been
cheated. Yes, the entire congregation had been
cheated of its Rosh Hashanah call, because of
clumsy, halting Jacov.

Alone in his room at last, Jacov felt too miserable
even to weep. The steady, flowing ache in his body
was worse than hunger. Though his parents tried to

speak to him, his mind would grasp no other thought but the knowledge of his failure and disgrace.

At last, when the night had grown cold and dark, there came a knocking at the door. Jacov heard soft, murmuring voices. Then he was called, and to his amazement, there in his parlor stood the rabbi himself.

Speechless and trembling, Jacov tried to force himself to meet the rabbi's gaze. He could not. Surely the rabbi would now tell him that another must be chosen to blow the shofar at the close of Yom Kippur day. Such a thing had never happened before. Always, the same person held the honor for both holy days. The rabbi would speak kindly, but the result would be that on Yom Kippur day Jacov would sit among the congregation, his face burning with shame.

To Jacov's surprise, the rabbi spoke softly, urgently, and for a long time. His words began to penetrate beyond Jacov's misery. Soon the rabbi's words began to warm him, until he was filled with a great joy. Jacov and the rabbi now shared a secret that on Yom Kippur day would be revealed.

Ten days passed—the ten days of awe and atonement, when Jews make their peace with themselves and their fellow men. Throughout the ten days, Jacov became more than ever the target for sly glances and cruel remarks. It took all Jacov's strength to keep his promise to the rabbi and to remain silent.

Some of the villagers came to the rabbi to complain, to ask what would be done, to demand that another person be chosen to blow the shofar on Yom Kippur, the holiest of days.

The rabbi answered them all with a mysterious smile.

Two days before Yom Kippur it became known that the rabbi had set out on a journey to the city and would not return until the eve of Yom Kippur.

Such a journey during these holy days! Some members of the congregation pursed their lips and clucked their tongues—had the rabbi lost his senses?

Some even questioned Jacov, but again, true to his promise, Jacov remained silent. The mystery only grew when the villagers saw the rabbi returning from his trip, tired but happy, carrying a strangely shaped parcel under his arm.

At last came the day of Yom Kippur. This time Jacov sat among the congregation. His cheeks burned as he knew people were asking themselves, "Who? Who shall blow the shofar now?"

Perhaps, they thought, the rabbi would not announce the name of the honored person until the shofar was to be sounded. Then that one would walk up, head high, to take his place on the bemah, to blow the shofar for all to hear and admire.

All day long the service continued. When the time came at last for the final sound of the shofar, the congregation turned as one toward the rabbi. Each shared the same thought. What will our rabbi do now? Whom shall he choose? Will he admit before everyone that it was a mistake to choose that boy Jacov?

The last prayer was spoken. For a long minute the rabbi stood at his pulpit gazing out at everyone. At last he spoke in a voice so low that the people had to strain to hear.

"We shall now have the blowing of the shofar," he said. "On Rosh Hashanah," he continued, "when our ears were eagerly turned to hear the loud cry of the shofar, we heard instead a small, soft cry. Next, there was no sound at all, but only silence."

He paused, studying the upturned faces before him. Then he went on. "I have thought about this happening," he said, "and it has occurred to me that there are times when God wishes us to be silent, that we may listen to that soft, small voice inside us that tells us what is right and pure and just."

Now the rabbi's voice rose. "Our friend Jacov gave us such a moment of silence on Rosh

Hashanah day. Who can say that this silence was not pleasing to God? Jacov performed his duty with love, and so do we receive it. For it is written, 'I desire love, not sacrifice.' Love for each other and for God is more important than ritual."

The rabbi smiled and continued. "But today," he said, "to seal our new year, we shall hear the glorious sounds of the shofar. Jacov! Please come up to the bemah."

Smiling broadly, Jacov strode up to the bemah. He took the shofar and held it to his lips. He glanced at the rabbi and gave a slight nod.

Now a different murmur swept over the congregation as everyone shared a smile, an exclamation of surprise and delight, for on the bemah beside Jacov stood the rabbi, and he, too, held a shofar to his lips. Together the two horns were sounded. The people felt the thrilling, stirring notes, rising, calling, proclaiming that on this day a new year was begun, a new time was ushered in, a time of love for one's fellows and nearness to God.

The two shofars together called out more brilliantly than ever before, and none could say which shofar it was that gave the call so clearly.

At last all had to agree it was the harmony of

the two that made it—a sound to remember.